To Cylus
B Malachai
♡ Rinae
Johnson

Hidden Dragons

RENAE JOHNSON

ILLUSTRATED BY
JAMES HEIRMAN

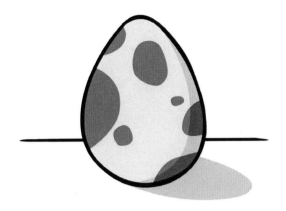

For Aries.

There once was a good wizard named Kablooey, Louie for short.

Louie loved to walk his dragon, Driscoll.
Sometimes he would ride on his
dragon's back, but Driscoll was
too young to fly yet.

Louie's little dragon was as curious as a cat and loved eating melon. This was a bad thing because they lived too close to the evil King Krabby's garden.

One day, Driscoll jumped over the king's wall and ate his fill of melons. One of the king's men saw the little dragon and informed the king.

The evil king declared war
on all dragons.

Louie was very afraid for his best friend
and dragons everywhere.
He knew he couldn't fight the king.
Louie was only one person.

He went to his friends and told them what happened. His friends were also afraid for their pet dragons as well, especially Klumpy.

Klumpy was a pig farmer. His young
dragon was raised with pigs. Warty loved
to wallow in the mud, roll like a gator
and bury his face in the muck.

Klumpy had given up on daily dragon
bathing and let Warty be happy amongst
the flies that danced around his scaly head.
He couldn't let the king hurt his Warty.

Chester, a freelance court jester, was currently unemployed. His best friend was his pet dragon Flexo.

Flexo was a spunky young pup full of tricks he'd learned for treats. He could roll over, sit, fetch and light a candle with a whistle.

When Louie told his dear best friend Neena, she spat at his feet, drew her sword and vowed to fight to the death for her pet dragon, Spike.

With Spike standing tall in Neena's
shadow, they looked like a proud army
waiting to defend the dragon race.
They almost gave Louie hope.
But he knew better.

The troops would be marching. They would attack at dawn. If Louie did nothing, their dragons, and dragons everywhere, would be defeated.

Louie knew it was his fault for letting his dragon, Driscoll, eat the melons. Now all dragons would perish. He loved Driscoll more than his own life but his friends, and everyone he could think of, loved their dragons just as much.

Louie was under a terrible weight. If he went to the king and tried to reason with him, maybe King Krabby would accept his dragon, Driscoll, and leave the rest of the dragons alone. It hurt poor Louie deeply but maybe he could save the others.

In the night, the wizard snuck into
the castle and found the king sleeping
in his chamber.

He woke him and pled with him to spare
the other dragons since it was his
Driscoll who ate his melons.

But the king saw how much the wizard
loved his dragon and realized how much
the dragons were loved by everyone
and grew jealous.

He wanted to be the object of their devotion and he would gain their loyalty through their fear and respect. He declared, "All dragons will die at dawn!"

Louie gathered his friends and all the dragons from everywhere.

They filled the village around a large fire
and tried to formulate a plan.

At dawn, they faced evil King Krabby and his army. Neena drew her sword.

But just as they were surrounded,
outnumbered, Louie knew
what he must do.

So he raised his wand high and with
a magic spell, he lifted all the dragons
in the air and shrunk them.

He put them into the swarm of flies
around Warty's head. Hidden forever,
dragonflies were born and survive,
even to this day.

The End.

Made in the USA
Middletown, DE
01 May 2021